Dragon
Trouble

Crabtree Publishing Company
www.crabtreebooks.com

PMB 16A, 350 Fifth Avenue
Suite 3308
New York, NY 10118

612 Welland Avenue
St. Catharines, Ontario
Canada, L2M 5V6

Lively, Penelope, 1933-
  Dragon trouble / Penelope Lively ; illustrated by Andrew Rowland.
    p. cm. -- (Yellow bananas)
  Summary: Peter's birthday gift to his grandfather turns out to be much
more unusual, and much more trouble, than either of them could have
guessed.
    ISBN 0-7787-0941-8 (RHC) -- ISBN 0-7787-0987-6 (pbk.)
    [1. Grandfathers--Fiction. 2. Dragons--Fiction. 3. Cornwall (England
:County)--Fiction. 4. England--Fiction.] I. Rowland, Andrew, ill. II.
Title. III. Series.
  PZ7.L7397 Dq 2003
  [Fic]--dc21

2002009613
LC

Published by Crabtree Publishing in 2002
Published in 1999 by Egmont Children's Books Limited
Text copyright © Penelope Lively 1984
Illustrations copyright © Andrew Rowland 1999
The Author and Illustrator have asserted their moral rights.
Reinforced Hardcover Binding ISBN 0-7787-0941-8 Paperback ISBN 0-7787-0987-6

Dragon Trouble

Illustrated by Andrew Rowland

PENELOPE LIVELY

YELLOW BANANAS

Dedicated to Mom and Dad

and number 49 with jam

A.R.

Chapter One

THERE WERE DRAGONS in England, once.
Hundreds of years ago. Or maybe thousands. It
could be that there still are, from time to time
– just the odd one, here and there. Anyway,
this is what happened to a boy of nine called
Peter, last summer.

He was spending his summer vacation with
his grandfather, in a small town somewhere
around the middle of Cornwall, in England. It
was an ordinary little gray stone town with
houses and shops and a market square – not
the sort of place where you'd expect to find
unusual things happening.

Peter's grandfather, though, was less ordinary.
He lived by himself in a wonderful messy
cottage with a canary in a cage and two rabbits
in a cage in the garden.

When Peter went to stay with him they
did whatever they both felt like and had french
fries for every meal. Sometimes they stayed in
bed until lunchtime and other days they played

card-games all day and once they decided to
make a five-foot model airplane and stayed up
all night doing it. I have to tell you that it all
came apart the next day, but they both felt it
had been worth it.

"Don't forget to buy Grandpa a card for his birthday," Peter's mother had said before he left. The day before the birthday, though, Peter decided that just a card would not do for such an excellent grandfather. He went off by himself into town to look for a present, it would have to be a very special present.

Tobacco? No, that was unhealthy. Chocolates? A corkscrew with a handle in the shape of an anchor? An ashtray with a map of Cornwall on it? Nothing he saw seemed right at all. He wandered into the town square. It was market day and there were fruit and vegetable stands, shirt and jeans stalls, and venders selling dog food and birdseed, and large crowds. There was also a junk stall at which Peter stopped. This was more promising. He thought about buying a ship in a green glass bottle, but it was much more than he could afford. An old wind-up gramophone would have been just the thing, but that was also expensive.

Then he caught sight of one of those glass domes on a stand that usually have a couple of stuffed birds on a branch under them. This one had a twig nest instead, and inside the nest were two large reddish speckled eggs.

As soon as Peter saw it he knew that this would be the perfect present. It might not be what Grandpa had always wanted, but he would want it as soon as he saw it. It was not too expensive. It had been reduced to two dollars because the glass was cracked and there were several chips out of the stand.

Peter bought it.

He was absolutely right: Grandpa was thrilled. "Now that's what I call a present," he said. "Original. Not your ordinary box of handkerchiefs or package of pipe cleaners. Just the thing for my mantelpiece."

So the glass dome was put in the center of the mantelpiece, and that evening, since it was very chilly, Grandpa lit a fire and he and Peter sat in front of it and ate fish and chips off their knees and admired Peter's present. "I'm sure it's an antique," said Grandpa. "A hundred years old or so, I figure."

Chapter Two

IT WAS PETER who came down first in the morning. He pulled back the curtains and had a look at the rainy weather and then glanced across the room at the glass dome.

Underneath it, something was moving. He stood still and stared. Impossible! He moved closer.

The eggs were gone. In their place were two small lizard-like creatures scratching frantically at the glass. For a few moments Peter gazed in amazement. Then he rushed upstairs to fetch Grandpa. Together they inspected the creatures more carefully. They were about five inches long. They had green scales blotched with red, legs with tiny claws, long tails with ends barbed like an arrow, and very small . . .

"Wings!" said Grandpa, putting on his glasses. "Would you believe it! Wings – no two ways about it!"

The creatures continued to scratch at the glass. "They look like," said Peter, hardly daring to breathe it, "DRAGONS!"

Grandpa nodded. "You've put your finger on it. What we've got here, to my mind, is a pair of young dragons. Extraordinary! It must be the heat of the fire that did it. Those eggs must have been laid away in some cold attic all these years. Bring them into the heat and they hatch. It's a wonderful thing, nature."

Clearly, they could not leave the dragons where they were. Apart from everything else, there would not be enough air for them under the glass. Grandpa found an old cardboard box which they lined with newspaper. Very carefully they lifted the glass dome from its base and tipped the creatures into it.

"Question is," said Grandpa, "what do we feed them?"

This turned out to be a problem. They tried
bread crumbs, bird food, bananas, and lettuce,
all of which the dragons ignored. They
retreated to the end of the box and sat there
forlornly. It wasn't until Grandpa and Peter had
their lunch, which was fish fingers and fries,
that they perked up. They began to sniff and
scratch at the sides of the box. Peter chopped
up a piece of fish finger and offered it to the
dragons. They devoured it.

The dragons grew quickly. After a week or so they were getting too big for the box. Grandpa repaired an old rabbit cage and moved the dragons into the garden and put them in the cage. They ate a package of fish fingers every day, with a can of salmon as an occasional treat. The dragons would eat nothing else, except giant prawns, which they ate whole, whiskers and all.

Peter and Grandpa were extremely proud of them. "You can keep your budgies and your cats and your dogs," said Grandpa. "I like an unusual pet. And these beat everything."

The dragons, admittedly, were not especially cuddly pets. They did not like being petted and hissed when disturbed. But they were very handsome. Their scales were now a rich grass-green decorated with reddish-brown spots. They had fine crests along their necks and their tails swished and curled. Their wings were transparent and large enough now to flap. They would sit in their cage preening and flapping and nibbling fish fingers.

Given all this, I suppose what came next was inevitable. Grandpa decided to exhibit the dragons at the town's annual pet show.

Chapter Three

THEY ATTRACTED IMMEDIATE attention. And caused instant trouble. "What are they, for heaven's sake?" exclaimed the lady in charge of arranging entries.

"Well," said Grandpa, "you've got a point there. I can see they don't fit in with Dogs or Cats or Cage-birds. Reptiles, maybe?"

Eventually, after a great deal of talk among the judges, the dragons were entered in the Miscellaneous Class, along with some tortoises, a tank of newts, two parrots, and a grass snake.

They were a great success. People crowded
around the cage peering through the wire
netting at them and exclaiming. The dragons
appeared to enjoy the attention. They strutted
up and down and played together. They were
now almost the size of rabbits.

The trouble started when it came to the
judging. Two of the three judges wanted to
give them First Prize but the third objected
strongly, on the grounds that nobody knew
what to call them. Finally a vote was taken.

The dragons were given a red ribbon, which Grandpa pinned proudly to the hutch.

The awkward judge, a round woman whose poodle had failed to win a prize in the Dog Class, remarked loudly that the things looked to her like something that ought to be in a museum and she wouldn't be surprised if they carried terrible diseases. She tapped the cage with her umbrella and then sprang backwards with a shriek. There was a sizzling sound and a smell of scorching.

The dragons had learned to spit flames. Very small flames, mind you, but flames all the same. Grandpa and Peter took them home in a hurry, before people could ask any more questions or make any more comments. On the way Grandpa bought a fire extinguisher.

"Just in case they were provoked. I figure they'll settle down again once we get them back." He spoke severely to the dragons, who now looked as innocent as lambs.

There was a short piece about them in the paper, with the heading LOCAL PENSIONER'S MYSTERY PETS. Grandpa had mixed feelings about this. He thought the photograph of himself was not flattering and he was worried that it would arouse too much curiosity. "There's no limit to how nosy people can be. You take my word for it. Jealous, too. That's what was up with that woman. Plain jealous. Her with her poodle done up like a lamb chop. Next thing, we'll have everyone wanting what we've got. And I'm not breeding them. I've had enough trouble that way with rabbits."

LOCAL PENSIONER'S MYSTERY PETS.

Chapter Four

GRANDPA WAS RIGHT to be worried, as it turned out. Three days later there was a knock at the door and on the step stood a man in uniform who said he was the Pest Control Officer and he had reason to believe that there were some unusual animals in the house. Grandpa and Peter stared at him in alarm.

"Lizards of some sort, is it?" continued the Pest Control Officer. "The name's George, by the way." He held out a printed card to Grandpa. "Mr George. Won't take a minute, but it's my job to check up. All right if I come in?"

They let him in and took him through to the
backyard. There was nothing else they could
do, really. Mr. George squatted down in front of
the cage and studied the dragons.

There was silence.

"Ah," said Mr. George. "Yes. I see. A pair
of . . . um . . . A pair of those things."

There was a glint, now, in Grandpa's eye.
"What," he said, "counts as pests?"

Mr. George stood up. "Rats. Mice.
Cockroaches. Black beetles. Wasps."

"And are what we've got in that cage any of those?" continued Grandpa.

"Strictly speaking," said Mr. George, "no."

"Then," said Grandpa triumphantly, "what's wrong with us keeping them?"

Mr. George thought about it.

"Strictly speaking," he said again, "nothing." He cast a doubtful look down at the dragons. "But they're a bit odd, you must admit. What . . . um . . . what exactly would you call them now?"

"Dragons," said Peter, before he could help himself.

Mr. George laughed. He patted Peter on the head. "Got quite an imagination, your grandson, hasn't he?" he said to Grandpa. "Well, we'll leave it at that for now. But I'll have to make up a report. Keep them under control. They look to me as though they could give you a terrible bite."

As soon as he had gone Peter and Grandpa heaved sighs of relief. It had been a dangerous moment, they agreed. "Someone's been snitching," said Grandpa darkly. "That woman with the poodle, I bet. Or one of the nosy-parkers on the street. Best thing we can do is lie low or else . . ."

"Else we might not be able to keep them," said Peter anxiously.

Grandpa nodded.

But the worst was still to come.

Chapter Five

A COUPLE OF days later Peter went out in the evening to feed the dragons and found to his horror that the cage was empty. Part of the wire netting front had been ripped away, evidently by strong little dragon claws. He and Grandpa searched the garden but there was no sign of them. They remembered with alarm that lately the dragons had been flapping their wings more and more, like fledglings about to take off. Had they flown away?

Grandpa shook his head sadly. "I don't know how they're going to manage on their own. How are they going to let people know that they like to eat fish fingers and nothing else?"

"Or canned salmon,"added Peter.

They searched the house, just in case, and then came outside again. And then, both at once, they noticed a curious noise coming from the neighbor's garden. A sound of splashing.

"What's Mrs. Hammond up to?" said Grandpa, frowning. Mrs. Hammond was the next door neighbor.

"But she's away!" Peter exclaimed. "Don't you remember – she asked us to water her tomatoes for her?"

They dashed to the fence and looked over. In the middle of Mrs. Hammond's garden was her most treasured possession, a large pond covered with water-lilies and bulrushes and filled with fat goldfish.

And there at the edge of the pond was one
of the dragons, contentedly munching on a
goldfish that it held in its front claws. Even as
they watched, the second one rose from a
clump of bushes, whooshed up into the air
with an unsteady flapping of wings and
plunged straight down into the pond. A few

seconds later it rose to the surface, scrambled
out, shook itself like a dog and settled down to
eat the goldfish that it, too, was now clutching.

"She's going to be *furious*!" cried Peter.

Grandpa was already rushing into the house.
He came out with a piece of green nylon garden
netting and a bucket. "Quick! Over that fence!"

Peter scrambled over and set
about the difficult business of catching
the dragons. Grandpa watched anxiously
from the other side and shouted words of
advice. The dragons scuttled around the
pond hissing angrily and sometimes spitting a
few feeble flames. From time to time they
took off and flapped a few yards across
Mrs. Hammond's lawn before flopping to

the ground. Evidently they weren't very good
at flying yet. At last Peter managed to net
them both and get them into the
bucket, which he passed over the
fence to Grandpa. There were
only three goldfish left in
the pond.

They put the dragons
back in the cage, where
they huddled into the
corner still hissing
quietly. Peter and
Grandpa hurried off to
the pet store on Main
Street and they bought
the entire stock of goldfish.

"Think she'll notice the
difference?" asked Peter when
he had emptied them into Mrs.
Hammond's pond.

Grandpa shook his head. "I doubt if
a person gets what you might call close
to a fish."

Chapter Six

THAT EVENING THEY took a long hard look at the situation. Things could not go on like this.

"You know something?" said Grandpa. "I think I know what it is we've got out there. What we've got is a pair of sea-dragons. Fish-eaters, see? I should have realized it before."

"Do you think they're full-size yet?" asked Peter.

Grandpa shrugged. "Maybe, maybe not. But one thing I'm clear about; they're getting out of hand. They're not the sort of thing you can keep in your backyard forever."

The more they thought about it the more it seemed to them that there were only two things they could do. They could give the dragons to a zoo. Or they could let them go.

"They'd hate it in a zoo," said Peter. "Being stared at all the time. And fed peanuts. But where could we let them go?"

"Where they ought to be," said Grandpa. "Their natural habitat. The sea."

And so the great plan was hatched. It took a lot of working out. They would have to take the dragons to the coast by bus since Grandpa did not have a car. Then they would have to find a beach with rocky cliffs to release the dragons.

They borrowed a cat carrier from a neighbor (Grandpa spun a story about having to take his rabbits to the vet), got the dragons into it, with some difficulty, and set off. The bus journey was tricky; the dragons rumbled around in the carrier so that Grandpa and Peter had to talk loudly to drown out the noise. But at last they reached the coast and set off for a beach where Grandpa knew there were cliffs dropping down into the sea.

There were a lot of people on the beach at the foot of the cliffs. Grandpa and Peter stood at the top of the path that led down to the sea and watched for a few minutes.

"It'll be all right as long as we can let them go quickly," said Grandpa. "Straight out to sea and no nonsense."

They opened the cat carrier. Peter pushed it near the edge of the cliff. The dragons stuck their heads out and flapped their wings.

They climbed onto the edge of the carrier and flapped their wings faster.

"That's it," said Peter. "Shoo! Go on – fly!"

And the dragons took off. They soared upward and then . . . oh, horrors! . . . they began to sink slowly toward the beach. They spun and flapped and fluttered down at last upon the sand. Peter and Grandpa gave one look, and set off at once in a hurry down the steep path to the beach.

They got to the spot where the dragons had landed and began to search for them. People were sitting around having picnics or tanning or reading newspapers. There was no sign of the dragons.

Suddenly Peter caught sight of one of them. It was sitting beside someone's picnic basket contentedly munching a tuna sandwich. The other one was stretched out on some children's sandcastle, sunning itself.

Peter rushed forward to grab them at the same moment as the owner of the tuna sandwich turned around and gave a loud scream. "Excuse me!" Peter panted. "My dog . . ." He snatched up the dragon just as the man was reaching for his glasses. He

seized the other one and popped them both into the cat carrier, which Grandpa was holding open. Several people were now staring at them and muttering. They rushed to the cliff path.

At the top Grandpa said grimly, "One more try. Or it's the zoo for the pair of them. We've done our best."

A breeze had sprung up. Perhaps that helped, or perhaps the dragons simply got better at flying after a little practice. Anyway, this time they soared upward and stayed up, floating and flapping over the beach and the people and out over the water. "That's the spirit!" cried Grandpa. Peter clapped and waved.

The dragons whisked their tails and swooped in circles. Their scales caught the sun and glittered until after a few minutes all Peter and Grandpa could see were two twinkling spots of light. And as they watched, the two spots plunged down suddenly into the sea, and then sprang up out of it again in a gleaming shower, and then down and up again . . .

"They're fishing!" cried Peter. Then he and Grandpa turned away and began to walk slowly back to the road to catch the bus.

Maybe those were the last dragons in
Cornwall. Maybe not. There's no telling. As
Grandpa said, nature is a wonderful thing.

YELLOW BANANAS

Don't forget there's a whole bunch of Yellow Bananas to choose from: